TOO
Small
Tola

D0928344

Books by the same author

Anna Hibiscus
Hooray for Anna Hibiscus!
Good Luck, Anna Hibiscus!
Have Fun, Anna Hibiscus!
Welcome Home, Anna Hibiscus!
Go Well, Anna Hibiscus!
Love from Anna Hibiscus!
You're Amazing, Anna Hibiscus!

The No. 1 Car Spotter
The No. 1 Car Spotter and the Firebird
The No. 1 Car Spotter and the Car Thieves
The No. 1 Car Spotter Goes to School
The No. 1 Car Spotter and the Broken Road
The No. 1 Car Spotter Fights the Factory

For younger readers
Anna Hibiscus' Song
Splash, Anna Hibiscus!
Double Trouble for Anna Hibiscus!
Baby Goes to Market
B Is for Baby

Non-fiction
Africa, Amazing Africa: Country by Country

TOO Small Tola

Atinuke

illustrated by

ONYINYE IWU

WALKER
BOOKS

Dedicated to Lani-Grace,
who is also small but mighty!
A.

For Mum, Dad, Junior, Alessia and Francis,
thanks for supporting my dreams,
this one is for you.
O.I.

This is a work of fiction. Names, characters, places and incidents are either
the product of the author's imagination or, if real, are used fictitiously.

First published 2020 by Walker Books Ltd
87 Vauxhall Walk, London SE11 5HJ

2 4 6 8 10 9 7 5 3 1

Text © 2020 Atinuke
Illustrations © 2020 Onyinye Iwu

The right of Atinuke and Onyinye Iwu to be identified as author and illustrator respectively of this work has
been asserted by them in accordance with the Copyright, Designs and Patents Act 1988

This book has been typeset in Stempel Schneidler

Printed and bound by CPI Group (UK) Ltd, Croydon CR0 4YY

All rights reserved. No part of this book may be reproduced, transmitted or stored
in an information retrieval system in any form or by any means, graphic, electronic
or mechanical, including photocopying, taping and recording, without prior written
permission from the publisher.

British Library Cataloguing in Publication Data: a catalogue
record for this book is available from the British Library

ISBN 978-1-4063-8891-6

www.walker.co.uk

MIX
Paper
FSC   FSC® C101537

CONTENTS

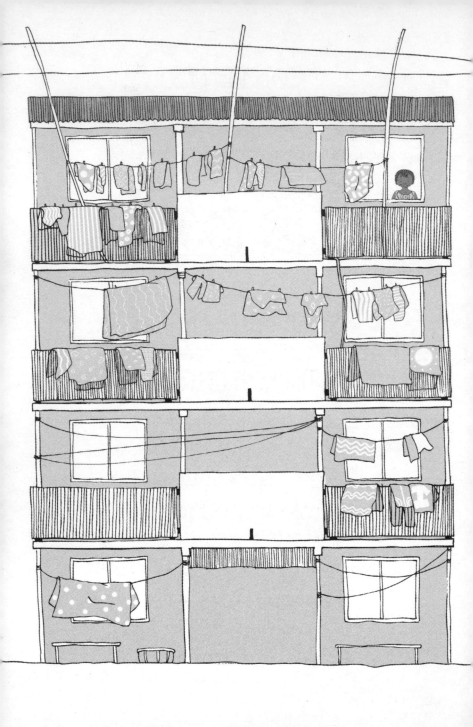

Dapo   Grandmummy   Moji

Tola

Too Small Tola

Tola lives in a run-down block of flats in the megacity of Lagos, in the country of Nigeria. She lives with her sister, Moji, who is very clever; her brother, Dapo, who is very fast and Grandmummy, who is very-very bossy.

Tola is the youngest in her family. And the smallest. And everybody calls her Too Small Tola, which makes her feel too-too small.

"Tola!" shouts Grandmummy. "O-ya, shopping! Let's go!"

Tola looks at Grandmummy in surprise. Shopping isn't her job! She is far too small to carry shopping!

"Why are you standing there looking at me?" asks Grandmummy. "Hurry up!"

"But..." Tola starts to argue.

She looks at her sister, Moji. Moji is big. Big enough to carry a mammy-wagon load of shopping.

But Moji is sitting at her borrowed computer doing her homework. She is wearing one of her A* looks of concentration. Tola sighs. Everybody knows not to get in Moji's way when she is wearing an A* look.

What about her brother, Dapo? Dapo is fast. He could reach market faster than an okada taxi.

But through the open window, carried on air as hot as pepper soup, come the sounds of boys playing football.

"Goal!" the boys roar. Then they start to chant, "Da-po! Da-po! Da-po!"

Tola sighs again. Everybody knows that Dapo is fantastic at football – and useless at everything else. Grandmummy says his tactics for avoiding work are as good as his football tactics.

Tola looks at Grandmummy. She is wearing one of her "what-did-I-tell-you" looks.

"Just hurry up, Tola," she says.

Tola hurries to put the big shopping basket on her head. She does not want to upset Grandmummy. If Grandmummy is upset, soon everybody will be upset. Grandmummy passes on her moods faster than mosquitos pass on malaria.

Moji looks up from the computer screen.

"Too Small Tola!" She laughs. "You will fall down when that basket is full!"

Tola tightens her eyes at Moji.

"Don't mind her," Grandmummy says. "I need you to count the change so that

nobody cheats me. Nobody can count faster
than you."

Grandmummy turns back to Moji.

"If Tola is too small, you want to carry the
basket for her?" she asks.

Moji turns back to the computer screen.
Her A* look deepens.

Grandmummy shakes her head
but she says nothing.
Tola follows
Grandmummy
out of the flat, then
pokes her head back
inside.

"Moji Big Breasts!"
she shouts, and she
closes the door quickly.
Tola knows that will
make Moji as angry as a
soldier ant.

Grandmummy tiptoes past the other doors. Tola tiptoes behind her. But as soon as they pass the door of Mama Business, it opens.

Mama Business greets them.

"Good morning! Good morning! Where are you going?"

"Good morning, Mama Business," Grandmummy says.

Grandmummy hurries down the dusty concrete steps. Tola hurries behind her.

"You are going to market?" Mama Business calls.

Grandmummy races out of the crumbling block of flats. "Now that Mama Mind-Your-Own-Business has seen us, soon everybody will know where we are going."

Dapo looks up from his game.

"Too Small Tola!" he shouts. "That basket is bigger than you!"

Tola's eyes tighten again.

"Don't mind him," Grandmummy says.

She shouts to Dapo, "Do you want to carry it?"

Dapo dribbles the ball very quickly. Grandmummy sucks her teeth.

"Wait until I return!" Grandmummy shouts after him. "Then you will work!"

Dapo pretends not to hear. But Tola can see that he now looks nervous, nervous enough to miss the ball. *Good,* Tola thinks.

Tola follows Grandmummy onto the busy road next to the flats. The smell of the gutter makes her wrinkle her nose.

She follows Grandmummy under a flyover. The sounds of car horns blaring and hawkers shouting make her wiggle her ears.

She follows Grandmummy past the mall.
Tola reads the shop signs: KFC, SAMSUNG,
SHOPRITE. Ikeja City Mall has the finest of fine
shops. Cold air rushes out of the open doors and
makes them shiver.

"Oyinbo air," Grandmummy mutters. "Why
did those Tokunbos use juju to bring it here!"
She crosses herself.

Tola giggles. Grandmummy thinks that people who have been abroad use magic to bring the cold air back from overseas. But that cold air is just made by air conditioners. Even Tola knows that, Too Small or not!

Tola and Grandmummy cross the lanes of big traffic on the expressway. They walk down busy alleyways where every window opens onto a shop and you have to point to what you want. They step over green stinking gutters and squeeze past cars that are crawling along.

It is a long way to Mile 12 Market. But at last they are there! Hundreds of market women shout for people to come and buy their superior goods. Thousands of shoppers scream at the prices of those inferior goods. Tola thinks that Mile 12 Market must be the biggest and busiest place in the whole big and busy city.

Grandmummy sighs happily. She loves Mile 12. Tola sighs too. The long walk has made her tired.

"You are small," Grandmummy says suddenly, "but you are strong, like me."

Tola looks at Grandmummy in surprise. She had not realized that Grandmummy was small too. But now she sees it is true! Grandmummy is not much taller than her and that means that Grandmummy is small. Very small. But Tola also knows that Grandmummy is very strong.

Grandmummy can pound enough yams to feed a gathering of the Flats Association. She

can carry enough crates of soft drinks for a birthday party. She can even separate the big Ododi brothers when they are fighting. They do not call Grandmummy Mama Mighty for nothing.

And if Grandmummy is that small but that strong, then maybe Tola can be strong too!

Grandmummy buys huge yams. They are rough and dark on the outside and white and smooth on the inside. After Grandmummy boils and pounds them, eating them will be like eating white fluffy clouds.

Tola counts out the money for the yams. Then she counts the change. Grandmummy loads the heavy-heavy yams into Tola's basket and Tola grunts.

"Too heavy for you?" asks Grandmummy.

"No, Grandmummy," Tola lies. She is determined to be as strong as Grandmummy.

Grandmummy buys armfuls of leafy green vegetables bursting out of sacks. She buys tiny red chilli peppers overflowing from baskets. She buys stiff white stockfish piled into towers.

And each time Tola counts out the money.

She counts the change. Then Grandmummy loads the goods into Tola's basket. Lucky for Tola they are so light she cannot even feel them.

Grandmummy buys a big sack of rice from the back of a lorry loaded with hundreds of sacks.

Tola counts out the money. She counts the change. Then she looks at the big sack of rice.

Grandmummy chuckles.

"I will help you with this one," she says.

The rice seller lifts the sack onto
Grandmummy's head. Grandmummy groans.

"Too heavy for you?" Tola is worried.

"Not at all," Grandmummy lies.

Grandmummy's phone beeps. It is a text from
Dapo. Grandmummy cannot read, so she passes
the phone to Tola.

Grandmummy buys a packet of nappies. Tola counts out the money. She counts the change. Then Grandmummy puts the packet of nappies on Tola's head, underneath the basket.

"That should stop you jumping around," says Grandmummy.

Tola sighs again.

"Something wrong?" asks Grandmummy.

"Nothing, Grandmummy," Tola says. She is determined to be as brave as Grandmummy.

Grandmummy chats with the nappy seller. She tells her all about Moji's A* grades. The nappy seller reminds Grandmummy that she had predicted Moji would be clever back in the days when Grandmummy was buying nappies for her.

Grandmummy's phone rings again.

"You answer," she says to Tola.

This time it is Moji, crying loudly. Grandmummy snatches the phone.

...ds her all the way to the computer sellers.

...oints to a stall selling just one thing.

... is what we need," she says.

..."you sure?" Grandmummy frowns. "I have

...hased a mouse with anything like that

...n sure," Tola says. "Moji will not get A*

...ut one."

...K," sighs Grandmummy.

... when Grandmummy hears the price she

...ks.

...ou want to kill me!" she shouts at the seller.

...ed this thing so my granddaughter can

...A*. And because of that you

...t to rob me!"

...Grandmummy pretends to

...lk away until the seller shouts

...t a more reasonable price.

...la counts out the money.

...e counts the change.

"What happen? What
Grandmummy.

"It is the mouse!" Tola
"I'm having trouble with t
I finish my essay?"

"Don't worry!" shouts Gi
mummy. "We will be back
soon!"

"There is a mouse in
the flat," Grandmummy
explains to Tola. "Your sister
is frightened. She cannot
finish her homework."

Tola giggles.

"Follow me!" she says to
Grandmummy. "I know what we n

Tola leads Grandmummy throug
market and back into the alleyways.
past the plastic shoe sellers, past the b
sellers, past the fresh meat sellers.

She lea
Tola p
"That
"Are
never c
before.
"I ar
witho
"Ok
But
shrie
"Y
"I ne
get
war

wa
ou
To
Sh

Then she counts the change again. And again.
She looks at Grandmummy.

"It is short," she whispers.

"Are you sure?" Grandmummy asks.

Tola nods.

Grandmummy takes the change from Tola
and counts it herself.

Then Grandmummy eyes the mouse seller
like a chicken eyeing an ant. The mouse seller
busies himself tidying his stall.

"What is this?" Grandmummy waves the
handful of change under his nose.

"It is your change," the seller says, not looking
at Grandmummy.

"It is short!" Grandmummy growls like a lion.

"It is not short," the man says.

But Tola can see his legs tremble like an
antelope being stalked by a lion. Grandmummy
opens her fist.

"Count!" she demands.

Slowly the mouse seller counts the change. When he gets to the end, he takes two new notes from his pocket and adds them to the pile, then continues counting.

"It is correct," he says.

Grandmummy sucks her teeth. She narrows her eyes and mutters "tief" under her breath. She is still grumbling as she tucks the new mouse into her handbag.

"Too expensive to put into a basket," she says.

Just then Grandmummy's phone rings again.

Grandmummy glares. This time it is old Mr Obi, calling from one of the top flats.

"My television needs collecting from the repair stall," Mr Obi croaks.

Grandmummy splutters. She presses a button on the side of the phone. The phone goes dead. Grandmummy looks at the phone. Then she looks at Tola.

"Phone battery done die," Grandmummy says firmly. "I did not hear who was calling."

Tola giggles. Grandmummy nods.

"Enough is enough!" she says firmly. "O-ya, let's go!"

Tola follows Grandmummy through the alleyways.

Grandmummy mutters crossly, "How did he want me to carry it?"

Tola giggles again at the thought of Grandmummy walking along with a television balanced on top of the sack of rice on her head.

"You think it is funny?" she asks. "Maybe he wanted you to carry it. To add to your own tower!"

Tola's eyes widen at the thought of a television added to the bag of nappies and the heavy basket on her head.

Tola's face makes Grandmummy laugh.

Tola and Grandmummy laugh together. But they do not laugh for long. Tola's load is very heavy. Grandmummy's load is even heavier.

"We are strong," says Grandmummy. "But we are also small. Let us rest."

Tola and Grandmummy stop in one of the busy alleyways. They rest by a window selling cold soft drinks. They rest and drink well-well, until Grandmummy says,

"O-ya, let's go."

Tola lifts the bag of nappies back onto her head. Grandmummy helps her to balance the basket of yams and vegetables and chilli peppers and stockfish and the football glue on top. A passerby helps Grandmummy to load the sack of rice back onto her head.

And off they go.

Tola follows Grandmummy closely as they cross the busy expressway. She is afraid of the speeding Mercedes. And the convoys of cars with their screeching sirens. And the lorries piled so high with stone and timber that they sag and wobble as if they are about to collapse. Tola sighs hard when they are safely across.

Then Tola follows Grandmummy back past the mall. She reads more shop names – ADIDAS, ISTORE, SILVERBIRD CINEMA.

Grandmummy walks very fast. She does not like oyinbo air at-all, at-all. And she likes juju even less. Tola tries hard to keep up.

But they cannot walk fast
for long. By the time they
reach the flyover they have slowed right down.

Tola's load is very heavy. Grandmummy's load
is heavier.

"We are strong," says Grandmummy. "But we
are also small. Let us rest."

So underneath the flyover Tola and Grandmummy rest where the doughnut seller is frying
doughnuts. They rest and eat doughnuts well-
well, until Grandmummy says, "O-ya, let's go."

They lift their loads back onto their heads
and off they go. Now they walk very slowly.
But they cannot even walk slowly for long. By
the time they reach the busy road Tola stops.

This road leads to the flats. But they are still far.

"We are strong," Tola pants, "but we are also small."

"Let's rest," agrees Grandmummy.

Tola and Grandmummy rest at the ice-cream seller's bicycle beside the road. They rest and they eat ice creams well-well, until Grandmummy says, "O-ya, let's go."

They lift their loads back onto their heads and off they go. They walk along the busy road. Now Tola can see the blocks of flats and she knows that they are nearly home. Soon they see Dapo running towards them.

"Did you buy it? Did you buy it?" Dapo shouts.

Grandmummy eyes him. "Take the rice!" she barks.

Dapo opens his mouth to argue. Then he looks at Grandmummy's face. Dapo decides to take the rice.

Moji is waiting by their block of flats.

"Why so long?" she shouts.

"Help your sister with the basket and stop complaining," Grandmummy orders.

Moji looks at Grandmummy's face. She takes the basket from Tola and does not say another word.

Up the stairs they all go. Tola feels as light as a feather with only the nappies to carry.

She starts to sing her favourite D'banj song and shakes her bom-bom up the stairs.

Dapo turns to looks at her.
Moji narrows her eyes.

"Why are you
so happy?" Moji asks.
But Tola is too busy
singing to answer.

"Anyway," says Dapo, "that song is old."

But Tola does not care. She loves it and sings
loudly about Oliver Twist and Beyonce and
Omotola all the way up.

Inside the flat Grandmummy sits down
heavily on one of the chairs.

"It is good to rest," she says.

"Again," says Tola giggling.

"What are you laughing about?" asks Dapo.

"Where did you rest before?" Moji asks.

"Nowhere," says Tola.

"Tola," says Grandmummy firmly. "You should not lie to your sister."

"Where did you rest?" shout Moji and Dapo together. "Tell us!"

"Tell them, Tola," says Grandmummy. "You must obey your older siblings."

"OK." Tola grins. "We rested at the soft drink seller."

"Soft drinks!" Moji and Dapo shout.

"The one in the alleyway near the market," Grandmummy confirms.

"Then we rested at the doughnut seller," Tola continues.

"Doughnuts!" Moji and Dapo shriek.

"The one near the flyover," Grandmummy confirms.

"Finally we rested at the ice-cream seller," Tola says.

"Ice creams!" Moji and Dapo scream.

"The one who cycles up and down the road," Grandmummy confirms.

"Soft drinks, doughnuts, ice creams," Moji wails.

"Did you bring any for us?" Dapo asks hopefully.

Too Small Tola shakes her head. "According to you I am too small to carry much." She grins.

Moji and Dapo groan.

"From now on," Grandmummy says, "you better call her Too Strong Tola."

And Too Strong Tola flexes her small muscles and laughs.

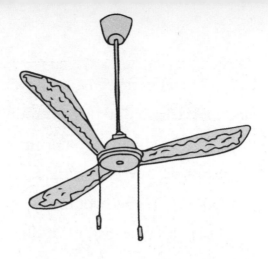

Small but Mighty

Tola lives in a run-down block of flats in the megacity of Lagos, in the country of Nigeria. Sometimes the electricity works. And sometimes it does not. Sometimes the water runs. And sometimes it does not. Once the lift worked. And now it definitely does not.

Tola wakes up. She is hot. She is sweating. She can hear Moji snoring in the bed next to her. And she can hear Dapo snoring on the floor. But she cannot hear the ceiling fan whirring round and around.

Tola sighs. The electricity is off. Again.

Tola sits up. It is still dark but Grandmummy is not in the bed. So she must have already gone to work. It is not time to get up for school but Tola needs to go to the bathroom.

So she gets up. She creeps out of the bedroom. She tiptoes past Dapo snoring on his mat on the floor.

There is only one room in their flat. A curtain divides the bedroom part of the room from the part of the room where they cook and sit and study. Room and parlour, Grandmummy calls it.

There is only one bed in the room. Tola and Moji and Grandmummy share the bed. Dapo cannot share it because he is a boy. So he sleeps on a mat on the floor.

Everything in the room is battered and old and cheap. Everything except for Grandmummy's earrings. Grandmummy's earrings once belonged to her mother's mother's mother's mother. Grandmummy says that when she wears them she can feel all those mothers blessing her. And that is worth more than the money she could get if she sold those earrings of pure gold.

Tola goes to the bathroom they share with other neighbours. It is a tiny room, like a wet room but with just a toilet and two taps. When they shower they take a bucket and position it under the taps. Then they use a jug to pour the water over themselves.

When Tola tries to flush the toilet it does not flush. She turns on a tap to wash her hands. But no water comes out. Tola sighs again. No electricity. And now no water.

It is one of those mornings when Grandmummy tells them to count their blessings.

"We could be living in the gutter under a cardboard box!" Grandmummy says.

"We could also be living in a big house on Victoria Island," Dapo grumbles.

Big houses all have generators and wells so they always have electricity and water. That is because the people who live there have big money. But Tola's family does not.

Grandmummy works hard selling groundnuts by the road six days a week. She would work seven but she takes Sundays off to thank God for all of her blessings.

One of her blessings is that Tola's father has a secure job. And he sends the money that pays for the rent of this one room.

"But if only he had a job here in Nigeria and not in the UK," Dapo would complain.

"And what secure job is there in this Nigeria?"

Grandmummy would always ask him.

Tola sighs for the third time. Then she creeps back to the bedroom and pokes Moji.

"Weytin?" Moji asks crossly.

"No water," says Tola.

Moji groans loudly and jumps up.

"O-ya," she says. "Let us go now or we will be late for school."

Tola nods.

She hates to be late for school. Teacher always does maths in the morning. And maths is her favourite subject.

On the floor Dapo is still snoring. Tola pokes Dapo with her foot. He does not move. Waking up Dapo is like trying to wake a car whose motor has died. No matter what you do, it does not respond.

Dapo is the only person who knows what to do with such a car. If he is not playing football he is sticking his head into cars to see what makes them work.

"Dapo!" Tola shouts.

Dapo just snores louder. Moji rolls her eyes. She pushes Dapo with her foot. But he just rolls over.

Moji sucks her teeth.

"Come on," she says to Tola. "We don't have time for him."

Under the table are six empty jerry cans waiting for mornings like this when the taps run dry – again.

Moji picks up a jerry can. She balances it on her head.

Tola puts an empty jerry can on her head too. She will fill it. But not to the top. She is not big like Moji.

Tola and Moji have not bothered to change

into their school uniforms. They are going to get hot and sweaty collecting water. So they just tie their wrappers tighter.

Then they leave the room and hurry down the dusty concrete steps. It is still cool outside. It is still dark. But the cockerels are beginning to crow and inside the flats kerosene lights are coming on.

"Hurry," says Moji. "Before everybody else gets here and we have to start queuing."

Tola and Moji hurry to the outside pump.

The taps in the flats are connected to water pipes coming from the government water authority. They often stop working.

The pump outside the flats is connected to a borehole that always has water. Water that has to be pumped and then carried up the steep stairs into the flats.

Moji pumps while Tola positions the jerry cans under the stream of water. When they are full, Tola helps Moji to lift hers onto her head. Moji helps Tola to lift her own.

Then they hurry as fast as they can back to the block of flats and up the stairs. As fast as they can with their necks aching and their knees buckling and their breath panting.

They have to collect enough water to flush the toilet. Enough water for Grandmummy to cook with when she comes home. Enough water for her to wash clothes with.

And that means the four empty jerry cans waiting on the floor of the kitchen still need to be filled. And without Dapo's help, they will be late for school. Tola hates being late for school. But Moji hates it even more.

Back in their room Dapo is still snoring. Moji narrows her eyes at him.

"Dapo!" she shouts.

He stops snoring. Then he starts again.

Moji steps up to his mat with the full jerry can still on her head. Tola watches.

Moji stands over Dapo and lifts the full jerry can from her head. Tola stares.

Moji opens the lid of the jerry can and sloshes water onto Dapo's head. Tola snorts.

Dapo leaps from his mat as if it were on fire! He stares around him wildly as if he is being attacked by hidden enemies.

Tola laughs. The jerry can on her own head wobbles but she cannot stop laughing.

Dapo's eyes focus on Tola. Tola stops laughing. She steps behind Moji. Moji faces Dapo like a tiger facing a crocodile.

"No water," she snaps. "Collect the jerry cans and let's go."

"If no water," Dapo growls, "what did you throw on my head?"

"Jus' help us!" Moji shouts.

"We called you," Tola says, "but you would not wake up."

"I was sleeping!" Dapo shouts. "How could I hear you?"

"Sleeping ko, sleeping ni!" Moji says. "You better hurry up and help us or we will all be late for school."

Dapo grumbles and he groans and he says that he will complain to Grandmummy but he picks up two jerry cans. Dapo and Moji rush out. By the time Tola gets to the stairs they have gone and there is only Mrs Shaky-Shaky waiting to go down the stairs.

"Good morning, Mrs Shaky-Shaky," Tola says politely.

"Good morning Tola," says Mrs Shaky-Shaky and she grips Tola's shoulder. Together they go slowly down the stairs.

Mrs Shaky-Shaky's legs are so shaky she has to grip somebody otherwise she might fall down.

Now Tola cannot hurry after Moji and Dapo.
Now she will be late for school.

Mrs Shaky-Shaky laughs.

"Look at us, Tola," she says. "We are the same
height. Maybe, like me, you will stay small."

Tola looks at Mrs Shaky-Shaky. It is true. They
are exactly the same height! This means that
some people never grow any taller. And maybe
one of those people is Tola!

"Don't let anyone tell you that you are too
small," Mrs Shaky-Shaky says as they reach the
bottom of the stairs. "One can never be too small."

"No, Ma," says Tola sadly, knowing it is not
true.

Mrs Shaky-Shaky smiles.
She pinches Tola's cheek
with a shaky hand.

"You are a good girl,
Tola," she says. "Thank
you for your help.

Now run or you will be late for school."

So Tola runs. But by the time she reaches the pump there is a long queue of people waiting with buckets and jars and jerry cans. Moji and Dapo are near the front.

"What is wrong with you?" Moji shouts at Tola when she takes her place at the back. "Now you will be late!"

One of the troublesome Ododi brothers joins the queue behind Tola. He heard what Moji shouted.

"What is wrong with her? What is wrong?" he shouts back.

"She's Too Small Tola! That's what is wrong with her!"

He laughs. And other people in the queue laugh too.

Tola presses her lips together. But she does not say anything. Nobody messes with the Ododi boys. Not even people bigger than her.

"Sorry, Tola," Moji whispers when she goes past with her full jerry cans.

Tola does not look at Moji. She does not answer her. If she did, she would cry. So she just keeps her eyes on the ground all the way to the pump. She has to work the heavy pump all by herself. Then she struggles to lift the heavy jerry can onto her head.

"Look at Too Small Tola!" the Ododi boy shouts. "So small she is practically useless."

Tola tries hard not to cry. But nobody laughs this time. Mrs Ronke steps forward to help Tola lift the can onto her head. But nobody says anything to the Ododi boy. Nobody messes with the Ododi brothers.

Tola turns back towards the flats and starts to walk. Her neck is aching, her knees are buckling, and she is panting.

And just as she passes the Ododi boy, Tola trips. She feels herself falling. The jerry can hits the ground and the lid comes off. Water pours out, onto the ground.

Tola hears the Ododi boy laugh. She sits up. The Ododi boy has his foot sticking out into the path. He tripped Tola! He tripped her up on purpose!

Mrs Shaky-Shaky is standing in the queue on her shaky-shaky legs. She looks at Tola but she does not say anything. Nobody in the queue says anything. Nobody messes with the Ododi brothers.

Tola picks up her almost-empty jerry can and joins the back of the queue again. She is crying now. Crying because she is so angry. And she does not even care that everybody can see her cry.

It is the Ododi boy's turn to fill his buckets. When he is done he turns back towards the flats. There is a big jeering smile on his face as he looks at Tola.

But just as he passes Mrs Shaky-Shaky the Ododi boy trips. He lands on the ground, hard. His buckets empty themselves.

People jump back and shriek as the water splashes them. Then the whole queue goes silent.

Everyone stares at the Ododi boy lying on the ground.

Then they stare at Mrs Shaky-Shaky's foot stuck out on the path.

Slowly people start to clap. They clap for the tiny shaky old lady who felled the big tough troublesome boy.

Tola stares. She stares at the small-small lady who took down the big bad boy just for her. Tola stops crying.

The Ododi boy leaps to his feet. He looks at Mrs Shaky-Shaky with her foot sticking out. Then he stands over Mrs Shaky-Shaky and bunches his fists.

Tola leaps forward. She leaps in front of Mrs Shaky-Shaky to shield her from the Ododi boy's fists.

Tola closes her eyes. She closes her eyes tight-tight-tight so that she cannot see his big-big fists and his angry-angry face.

With her eyes closed Tola sees nothing. But she knows that something is going to happen. There is a good reason that nobody messes with the Ododi brothers. Tola is trembling. But she does not run. She cannot leave Mrs Shaky-Shaky to be knocked down.

For some time nothing happens. Tola can see nothing. Tola can hear nothing. Eventually she takes a little peep.

Standing on one side of her is fat Mama Kunle. She must have left her place in the queue. On the other side is Mrs Abdul with baby Jide strapped to her back. They must have left their places in the queue too.

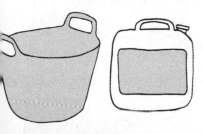

Then Tola sees old Mrs Ebiri, who is as
tough as stockfish, step forward. And huge Mrs
Raheen, who once took down an armed robber
with a yam pounder. And tiny Mrs Ambode,
who kills giant rats with only a broom.

They all leave their places in the queue and stand beside Tola and Mrs Shaky-Shaky.

Tola dares to look at the Ododi boy then. His eyes are flitting from one woman to another. Tiny Mrs Ambode takes one step forward.

And the Ododi boy steps back.

Mrs Shaky-Shaky pokes her shaky head around Tola.

"You are afraid of an old lady?" she asks. "Come on!" she says, doubling up her shaky-shaky fists.

Mrs Raheen rolls up her sleeves. And Mrs Ebiri unties her headscarf and ties it around her waist. Mama Kunle positions her legs wider. The women are ready to fight! The Ododi boy takes another step back.

Suddenly he turns and runs!

Mrs Shaky-Shaky starts to laugh. She laughs and laughs and all the women join in.

"If you try anything again," Mrs Shaky-Shaky shouts after the Ododi boy, "you will have me to reckon with!"

And she waves her shaky-shaky fists.

All the women laugh again. Then they readjust their clothing, pick up their buckets and jars and jerry cans, and resume their places in the queue.

Mrs Shaky-Shaky pinches Tola's cheek with a shaky hand.

"Remember what I told you," she says. "There is no such

thing as too small. And you are mighty. Just like your grandmother."

Tola rubs her cheek. She stares at the small figure of the Ododi brother, who is still running. Did she really help to scare him away?

Then Tola hears someone calling her name. It is Dapo. He is hurrying towards her, carrying the last two jerry cans.

"Give me your can," he says. "I will fill it for you."

Tola hands him the can.

"Now run!" Dapo says. "Or you will be late for school."

Tola smiles. She smiles at Mrs Shaky-Shaky. And she smiles at Dapo.

"Thank you!" she says, and then she runs.

Tola runs back to the flat. She fills a bucket half full with water from one of the full jerry cans. She carries the bucket and some black soap and a towel to the bathroom.

She uses a jug to pour water over herself, uses the soap to wash herself and uses the rest of the water to rinse herself. She dries herself with the towel and goes back to the room.

Moji is just leaving. She is wearing her smart white-and-blue stripy uniform with her tie. She has a rucksack on her back and smart shining shoes. In her hand she has a slice of bread.

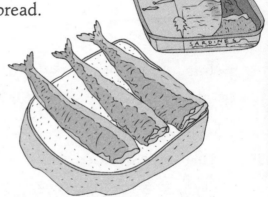

"There is bread and sardines on the table for you," she says as she bangs the door behind her.

Tola struggles into her uniform. It is not smart like Moji's. It is plain and brown. And she does not have smart shoes, just her old flip-flops. But she does not have a scholarship to help her go to a fancy school. Not like Moji.

Tola tries to ignore the bread and sardines so that she is not late. But she is too hungry. So she stuffs some into her mouth. Then she snatches up her bag and rushes out of the door.

On the stairs she passes Dapo. He has one jerry can on his head and two in his hands. With every step he has to stop and put down the cans he is carrying. Sweat is running down his face.

Tola looks at Dapo. She sighs. Then she points to one of the jerry cans and points to her head. Her mouth is too stuffed full of bread and sardines to speak. Dapo shakes his head.

"Jus' go!" he says.

So Tola goes. Dapo does not care about missing school. But she does. And he knows that. Tola will run all the way, but Dapo will linger, kicking a ball to any boy who is around, and poking his head into the engine of any car that has its bonnet open.

Tola runs down the stairs. She runs out of the door. She runs across the waste ground to the road. There are many rusty yellow danfo minibuses juddering along.

One stops. It is already jammed with people. But Tola squeezes in. The danfo starts with a jerk. It chugs off down the road. Soon they are at the street of Tola's school.

Tola jumps off the bus and runs up the street. She does not know if she is late or not. She does not have a phone, or even a watch. She runs to the school building and into her class.

The teacher is standing beside his desk. Children are crammed around tables in front of him.

"Tola Adebayo!" the teacher calls.

"Yes, sa!" Tola answers. She is in trouble now.

But then the teacher calls another name. Tola sighs with relief. Teacher is just calling the register!

Tola slips onto her chair. She smiles at her friend who sits next to her. She is not late. Not even one minute late! So she has missed no maths at all!

THIS HOUSE
IS NOT
FOR
SALE

Easter and Eid

Tola lives in a run-down block of flats in the megacity of Lagos, in the country of Nigeria. Soon it will be both Easter and the end of the Ramadan feast of Eid. Everybody in the flats is happy. Easter and Eid do not often happen at the same time and celebrations are all anybody is talking about.

"I am planning our Eid feast," says Mrs Abdul hungrily.

Mrs Abdul fasts during Ramadan and gives the money she usually spends on food to the homeless.

"And I am looking forward to shaking my palm leaves in the procession on Palm Sunday," says Mrs Shaky-Shaky.

"Me too!" says Tola.

"It will be a beautiful sight," agrees Mrs Abdul.

Tola is so looking forward to Easter. The whole family gets new clothes for Easter Sunday. And they process through the streets to church, waving their palm leaves and singing. It is always a wonderful day.

Tola and Grandmummy are busy planning their outfits. Tola wants ruffles on hers, but Grandmummy shakes her head. Ruffles take a lot of time to make so they cost more money than Grandmummy has got. Tola sighs. She has never had ruffles. And she has always wanted them.

Moji is bent over her schoolwork with her A* frown. And Dapo is complaining – as usual.

"How can I become a professional footballer," he moans, "without professional training?"

Tola, Moji and Grandmummy try to ignore him. They wish that he would be quiet. But Dapo has been moaning for weeks and he is not going to stop now.

"How am I supposed to train without a trainer?" he wails.

"Maybe you are good enough without training," says Tola.

Dapo opens his mouth to reply. But there is a knock on the door. It is Mr Abdul, the tailor.

"*Salam Alekum,*" Mr Abdul says politely.

"Peace be with you too," Grandmummy says.

"Come in, come in," she gestures.

Mr Abdul looks at Dapo, who has his head in his hands.

"That boy's muscles get bigger every time I see him," Mr Abdul says.

Dapo lifts his head. He smiles proudly.

Mr Abdul looks at Moji squinting at her screen.

"And this one is on her way to being a doctor, I hear," he says.

Moji looks up. She actually takes the time to smile too.

Mr Abdul looks at Tola, jumping up and down behind Grandmummy.

"And you are the little one who likes to count, are you not?" Mr Abdul asks.

Tola nods shyly. She smiles. Numbers are her favourite thing.

Last year Mr Abdul let her use his tape measure when he came to measure the family for their Easter outfits. Tola had measured everybody's waists and shoulders. And she had got most of the measurements right.

"Do you want to measure today?" Mr Abdul asks.

Tola nods again.

Mr Abdul hands her his tape measure.

"Go ahead," he says.

Dapo laughs. Moji raises her eyebrows. But Tola just ignores them.

"Don't pull the tape too tight," Mr Abdul
reminds her as she is measuring Grandmummy's
arms.

"Don't let the tape hang slack," he says as she
is measuring Moji's long legs.

"Don't forget around those arms," he adds as
she is measuring Dapo's broad shoulders.

Tola carefully writes down each and every
measurement on a piece of paper. And then
Mr Abdul measures exactly what she has just
measured.

And each and every measurement is exactly the same!

Mr Abdul looks at Tola in amazement.

"Tola! Tola!" he says. "This is wonderful. You must be the best measurer in Lagos!"

Dapo looks astonished. Moji looks startled. But Grandmummy nods as if she knew. Tola smiles shyly.

Then Mr Abdul turns to Grandmummy. "You have chosen the cloth?"

Grandmummy has. She has chosen green cloth with purple butterflies from the market. All their outfits will be made from the same cloth.

"Butterflies!" Tola had clapped her hands when she had seen it.

"I would have preferred BMWs," Dapo had complained.

Moji had said nothing. The only butterflies she noticed were the equations fluttering around in her head.

"Beautiful, beautiful," Mr Abdul says when he sees it. "You will all look very fine."

Mr Abdul goes off with the cloth and the measurements inside his head. He will sew their clothes in his flat downstairs. That is where he makes all his customers' clothes. And when they are ready he will return with them.

Tola looks out of the window and sees him cycling off to see another customer, his sewing machine strapped to the back of his big black

bicycle. Mr Abdul always takes his sewing machine with him, just in case he has to do repairs or adjustments for his customers.

But when Tola comes home from school the next day there is bad news.

"An okada motorbike overtook Mr Abdul," Grandmummy says. "He fell off his bicycle and broke his leg."

Tola gasps and claps her hand over her mouth.

"Luckily," Grandmummy continues, "the sewing machine was not damaged."

Tola is glad. At least with his sewing machine Mr Abdul can still work.

When Tola and Grandmummy go downstairs to visit Mr Abdul he is sitting cheerfully on the floor in front of his sewing machine. He is busy sewing green cloth with purple butterflies!

"Our clothes!" says Tola.

"Of course." Mr Abdul smiles. "I do not allow broken legs to spoil Easter!"

But in the kitchen Tola can see Mrs Abdul crying.

"Those okada drivers!" she wails. "They are too-too dangerous! The governor keeps saying they are banned but they are still everywhere. Everywhere! Now what will we do, Mama Mighty? What will we do?"

Grandmummy goes to comfort her. They talk for a long time.

"Mr Abdul can still make clothes," Grandmummy explains later, "but he cannot ride his bike around the city to take orders from his customers."

"Is that why Mrs Abdul was crying?" asks Tola.

"Shh!" says Moji. "I am trying to study."

Grandmummy ignores Moji.

"Yes," she says. "Mr Abdul's customers will have to get another tailor. And Mr Abdul will lose money."

"What about their Ramadan feast?" Tola asks.

Feasts cost money. Tola knows that.

"Shh!" says Moji again.

But Tola is too worried about Mr and Mrs Abdul to take any notice.

"They cannot miss their feast!" Tola cries. "They have been fasting for weeks!"

"Worse than that." Grandmummy is worried. "They might not be able to pay the rent."

"Oh no!" cries Tola.

"Be quiet, Tola!" shouts Moji.

"But, Mr Abdul!" Tola shouts back.

"If you are so worried about Mr Abdul, why don't you go and measure his customers yourself!" Moji says crossly.

Dapo laughs.

"Can you imagine?" he says. "Too Small Tola trying to ride that bicycle!"

Tola narrows her eyes at him. Dapo laughs even louder.

"I can see it now!" he snorts. "Those small-small legs trying to reach the pedals!"

"If you think it is so funny, then maybe you should ride the bicycle!" Tola shouts angrily. She punches his arm.

Dapo stops laughing. He rubs his arm.

"Did you see what she did to me?" he complains to Grandmummy.

Grandmummy says nothing. She looks at Tola, then she looks at Dapo. Then she looks back at Tola and rubs her fat hands together.

"Uh-oh!" says Dapo.

"It is a good idea," Grandmummy announces. "Tola can measure the customers. Dapo can ride the bicycle."

Tola stares at Grandmummy. *What?*

"What!" shouts Dapo. "I am not pedalling around and around on that heavy bicycle."

"Think of it as training," Grandmummy says, smiling.

"It's what you have always wanted." Moji smirks.

Tola giggles then too.

Dapo opens his mouth to argue.

"Think how big your calf muscles will grow," Grandmummy continues.

"It will be just like going to the gym," Moji joins in. "All day long."

"Oh no!" Dapo groans. "All the other boys will laugh at me."

Tola giggles again.

Then she thinks of herself on the back of that bike. And she thinks of all those strangers, all those strangers Grandmummy wants her to measure.

Tola stops giggling.

But when Grandmummy tells Mr Abdul the idea, and when he looks at Tola, and when he asks, "You will do this? You will do this for me?" then Tola remembers Mrs Abdul crying. And she remembers how

Mr Abdul is kind to everybody. So she takes a deep breath. And she nods her head.

"I am a lucky man!" Mr Abdul proclaims. "I have the best measurer in all of Lagos taking my measurements!"

And Tola manages a tiny-tiny smile.

Then Mr Abdul looks at Dapo.

"And with you in charge of my bike," he says, "it will be reaching record speeds."

Then Dapo manages a smile too.

Mr Abdul explains to Tola all about his customers – the fussy ones, the kind ones, the grumpy ones. Those who would offer them water, and those who would only complain.

Then Mr Abdul explains to Dapo about how to find all those customers. Those that live at the top of flats as tall as giraffes. Those who live at the bottom of alleyways that smell like hyenas. Those who live in mansions the size of a whole herd of elephants.

Then Tola takes the measuring tape and a small bit of paper and an even smaller bit of pencil from Mr Abdul. And Dapo and Tola get onto Mr Abdul's big black bicycle.
And off they go.

Grandmummy waves goodbye.

"Do a good job!" she shouts to Tola. "Look after your sister!" she shouts to Dapo.

Dapo pedals the bicycle along the bumpy road. There are potholes full of water and mud and stones. There are cars bumper to bumper honking their horns. Tola holds on tight.

Dapo stops at a small clean block of flats.

Outside it there is grass and big trees giving shade and flowers in pots. Tola stares. It looks nothing like their crumbling block of flats with its stained walls and the rough potholed bare earth around it.

A lady waves to them from a balcony.

"Enter! Enter!" she says. "Mr Abdul called to say that you were coming."

The lady offers them soft drinks. Then she
and her five children line up.

Tola measures the lady and writes down her
measurements. She measures the five children
and writes down each and every one of their
measurements. Mr Abdul would not have had to
write anything down. Mr Abdul cannot write.
But his memory is as long as an elephant's trunk.

Tola collects the drawings of the outfits that
the lady wants. And the lady gives her the cloth
that she wants the outfits to be made from.

And then they get back onto Mr Abdul's bike.

The lady and her children wave goodbye.

"Thank you! Thank you!" they shout. "We look forward to our new Eid clothes."

Dapo pedals away. Tola holds on tight. They cross the huge Third Mainland Bridge with its eight official lanes of traffic. It is the second longest bridge in Africa. Tola knows that from school.

Then Dapo pedals down the rocky, bumpy streets of Ikoyi. Here the gutters do not smell. And on either side of them are high walls topped with broken glass.

Dapo stops at some metal gates with a tiny intercom. The gates open by themselves to let them in.

Inside is a house as big as an oba's palace. It has shining white walls and thick white pillars holding up its balconies. A uniformed man comes out. He looks down at Dapo's dusty bare feet. He looks at Too Small Tola. Then he raises his eyebrows.

Tola pokes Dapo.

"Good morning," Dapo says. "We are Mr Abdul's assistants."

"Madam will only see Mr Abdul," the man replies.

"OK," says Dapo and starts to turn the bike around.

Tola pokes Dapo even harder.

Dapo sighs and says, "Mr Abdul has sent the best measurer in Lagos to measure her."

The uniformed man frowns. Then he marches back inside the house.

"Can we go now?" Dapo asks.

Tola shakes her head.

After a while a very
fancy woman comes out.
She is wearing fine clothes
and heavy gold jewellery
and her feet are spilling out
over tiny-tiny shoes. She
glares at Dapo and Tola.

"Before you touch me,"
she says, "you must wash
your hands."

Dapo opens his mouth
to argue. Tola pokes him
again.

She gets off the bicycle.
She washes her hands carefully at the garden
tap. Then she measures the woman. She writes
the measurements down. The woman calls her
servant to bring out some magazines. She shows
Tola two pictures of what she wants her outfit
to look like.

"Like this?" Tola points at the sleeves in one of the pictures. "Or like this?" She points at the sleeves in the other picture.

"No! No!" the woman shouts.

She turns the pages and shows Tola a different picture altogether. Tola ticks the sleeves in the third picture.

"Like this?" Tola points at the skirt in the first picture. "Or like this?" She points at the skirt in the second picture.

"No! No!" the woman shouts.

She turns the pages and shows Tola yet another picture. Tola ticks the skirt in the fourth picture.

"Like this?" Tola points at the neckline in the first picture. "Or like this?" She points at the neckline in the second picture.

"No! No!" the woman shouts.

She turns the pages and points to the neckline in a fifth picture. Tola ticks it.

It takes a long time and a lot of pictures until at last Tola thinks she knows exactly what the woman wants her outfit to look like. Tola wants to be sure that she makes no mistakes.

Dapo stands by the bike and scowls.

"Make sure you get it right!" the woman shouts, pushing the magazine at Tola, "or I will not pay!"

Tola nods. She gets back onto the bike with the magazine. And off they go.

When the big metal gates close behind them, Dapo says some words that Grandmummy has banned. Tola grins.

Now they have to go to Victoria Island. Dapo pedals down streets that are almost empty of cars. Instead there are shady trees. Tola cranes her neck and looks up. In the branches of the trees, birds sing and monkeys screech. She smiles. It is good to be away from the loud smelly traffic and the hot-hot sun.

Dapo stops at a house made of glass and metal. It is not like a house, Tola thinks. It is more like a shop showing off every fine-fine thing inside. Parked beside the house is a Lamborghini, a Porsche and a Jeep.

Dapo parks the bike next to the cars and stares and stares and stares. Next to football, Dapo likes cars best.

Afrobeat music blares out as soon as the front door opens. A man and a woman come out. The woman is wearing clothes so tight and shoes so high that her legs seem as long as a giraffe's. And the man's trousers are so low that his legs seem as short as a tortoise's.

Tola looks at them with her mouth open until the man coughs and Tola remembers why she is there.

"Tell Mr Abdul we want totally traditional outfits this time," the woman says. "*Ankara* for both of us."

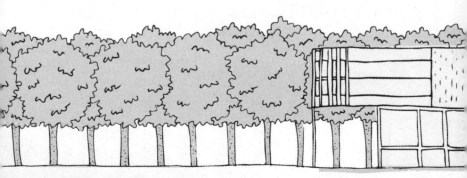

Tola nods in time to the music. Even her shoulders nod. She cannot help herself. She loves Afrobeat.

"You like it?" The man laughs.

Tola's body is still nodding.

"It is my tune," the man says, as if it was nothing.

This time Tola's mouth opens and closes in time to the music. This tune is famous! This man is famous! The man laughs.

"Measure me!" He laughs, opening his arms. "And I will sign your measurements."

Tola can't help clapping her hands. And Dapo

dances around the cars. The music has taken his body but his mind is still on those fine-fine cars.

At last they have measured every single person on Mr Abdul's list. Back they go along the shady roads of Victoria Island. Back along the bumpy roads of Ikoyi. Back over the Third Mainland Bridge with its more-than-eight unofficial lanes of cars and lorries and taxis and buses and limousines and motorbikes and minibuses and tankers and motorcades. Back past the bumper-to-bumper traffic of mainland Lagos. All the long hot way home.

When they get there Tola runs into Mr Abdul's room and parlour with all the cloth and all the measurements.

Mr Abdul claps his hands happily to see them. Tola shows him the measurements and he smiles. She shows him the magazine pictures and tells him what each customer wants and he nods.

She hands him the cloth.

Then Mr Abdul gets out his scissors.

"Are you sure, *habibi*?" Mrs Abdul asks, worried. "Are you sure the measurements are right?"

Tola looks worried then too. But Mr Abdul nods.

"I am as sure as sure can be," he says. "Tola's measurements are as good as my measurements."

Tola crosses all her fingers and all her toes.

Now every day Tola and Dapo ride around the city visiting shacks and chalets, mansions and markets, houses and hotels.

Dapo pedals
and pedals

and pedals. Tola measures
and measures
and measures.

And back at the flats Mr Abdul sews and sews and sews.

Then, just before Easter and the end of Ramadan, Tola and Dapo deliver all the clothes.

Tola's fingers are crossed so tightly that her hands ache. Her toes are crossed so tightly that her feet hurt. She is so nervous that even her stomach is crossed in a knot!

She watches and waits as each and every customer tries on each and every outfit. And all the outfits fit! Each and every one fits perfectly.

Even the large and fancy woman cannot complain.

Tola collects money from all of Mr Abdul's customers. And from the large and fancy woman she collects more than ten times as much money. Mr Abdul had warned Tola about that woman from the beginning. And he had told her what to charge her at the end. It was the price of rudeness, he said.

When they hand over the money to Mr Abdul, Mrs Abdul is so happy she cries and hugs them, and cries and hugs them again.

Tola and Dapo are happy too. Dapo's calf muscles are as big as the pillars holding up the Third Mainland Bridge. Tola's memory for measurements is as long as the lines of traffic that cross it. And most importantly, Mr and Mrs

Abdul have all the money that they need for their rent and for their Ramadan feast!

On Easter Sunday, Tola and her family will parade all the way to church with their palm leaves. And in the evening they will go to Mr and Mrs Abdul's end-of-Ramadan Eid feast. It will be a wonderful day.

Mr Abdul finishes Tola's new Easter outfit. He holds it up for her to see. Tola gasps and covers her mouth. All over her new Easter outfit are ruffles. The tiniest, cutest ruffles she has ever-ever seen!

Atinuke was born in Nigeria and spent her childhood in both Africa and the UK. She is the author of the bestselling Anna Hibiscus and No. 1 Car Spotter series, as well as *Africa, Amazing Africa: Country by Country*. She started her career as an oral storyteller of tales from the African continent; now she writes about contemporary life in Nigeria. Atinuke lives on a mountain overlooking the sea in West Wales. Visit her website at **atinuke-author.weebly.com**

\|/

Onyinye Iwu is Nigerian. She was born in Italy, where she spent most of her childhood, then moved to the UK when she was a teenager.

A teacher by day and an illustrator by night, Oyinye enjoys reading books, especially ones that make her laugh.